Illustrated by Khayala Aliyeva
Written by Anthony Pinto

ISBN: 978-1-957922-49-2
Edition: October 2022

For all inquiries, please contact us at:
info@puppysmiles.org

To see more of our books, visit us at:
www.PuppyDogsAndIceCream.com

This book is given with love...

To _____

From _____

For Bobby the Zookeeper's surprise Christmas treat,
his wife packed him something exciting and sweet!
Tucked under his sandwich sat a **Gingerbread Man**,
who was ready to throw a wrench in the holiday plan!

It'd be Bobby's first taste, these cookies rarely stay put,
and little did he know trouble would soon be on foot!
But Bobby was an expert at wrangling things into cages,
that's how he filled up his zoo for kids of all ages.

He was caught by surprise when the cookie came alive,
and flew from his lunchbox with a roll and a dive!
"What the what?!" Bobby yelled, as the cookie ran out of sight,
"Get back here!" He puffed, as he searched left and right.

Bobby ran after the treat, trying not to fall,
"Ha!" The cookie chuckled, escaping over the wall!
**"Run, run, run... As fast as you can,
Everyone wants a bite of the Gingerbread Man!"**

The cookie then darted into the nearest enclosure...
Straight into a rhino with horn worn from exposure.
"Well, don't you smell tasty..." The hungry rhino snorted,
"And you smell like gym socks!" The sly cookie retorted.

Swerving out of reach the cookie then zoomed,
unlocking the cage as his pastry voice boomed.
**"Run, run, run... As fast as you can,
Everyone wants a bite of the Gingerbread Man!"**

The next thing he knew, he landed in a snake pit,
"Salutationsss. You look scrumptiousss!" One of them spit.
"Well, you look like worms!" The gingerbread teased,
as he cleverly dodged the long snakes with ease.

"Ssstop right there!" The biggest snake hissed out,
"But the door was left open!" The cookie did shout.
"Run, run, run... As fast as you can,
Everyone wants a bite of the Gingerbread Man!"

Dashing into the next cage the nimble gingerbread jumped,
but slammed on the brakes just before he bumped.
Into a cheetah who was both spotted and fierce,
with teeth so sharp that his sweet dough would be pierced.

"Bet you taste great!" The cat meowed straight,
With no time for teasing, the cookie opened the gate.
**"Run, run, run... As fast as you can,
Everyone wants a bite of the Gingerbread Man!"**

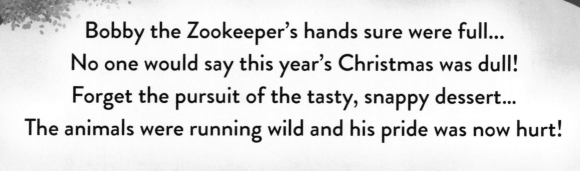

Bobby the Zookeeper's hands sure were full...
No one would say this year's Christmas was dull!
Forget the pursuit of the tasty, snappy dessert...
The animals were running wild and his pride was now hurt!

The cheetah caught up to the gingerbread before long...
But eating the treat that freed him? That would be quite wrong!

"I'm sure grateful you helped me escape and in turn,
I'll help you give others the freedom they yearn."

"Say, for a cheetah, you're alright! You know?
I'll teach you my ways. Let's give this plan a go!"
So the **Gingerbread Man** climbed on the cheetah's back,
to unlock all the cages with a loud, metal CLACK.

Cages swung open, and the animals were free,
They joined in a chorus to express all their glee.
**"Run, run, run... As fast as we can,
He can't catch us now... Thanks to the Gingerbread Man!"**

As the last creature disappeared, the zoo then became quiet,
poor Bobby was left with a gingerbread-free diet.
"I guess some things can't be caught," he said with a sigh,
Pesky little cookies and empty cages don't lie.

Claim Your FREE Gift!

 Visit:

PDICBooks.com/Gift

Thank you for purchasing

Everyone Wants a Bite of the Gingerbread Man

and welcome to the Puppy Dogs & Ice Cream family.
We're certain you're going to love the little gift
we've prepared for you at the website above.

Printed in the USA
CPSIA information can be obtained
at www.ICGtesting.com
LVHW060553251123
764762LV00019B/592